UNDULA.

Undula

BRUNO SCHULZ

TRANSLATED BY FRANK GARRETT

A SUBLUNARY OBJECT

Translation and afterword copyright © 2020 by Frank Garrett

Originally published as *Undula* under the pseudonym Marceli Weron in the journal *Świt*.

First edition. Second printing.

ISBN 978-1-7349766-5-6

Manufactured in the United States of America
Printed on acid-free paper

Design and typesetting by Joshua Rothes

Cover image "Undula w nocy" ["Undula at Night"] by Bruno Schulz, c. 1920-1922

Sublunary Editions
Seattle, WA
sublunaryeditions.com

CONTENTS

The translator acknowledges his indebtedness to scholar Lesya Khomych for her discovery of this previously unknown short story by Bruno Schulz published on January 15, 1922, under the pseudonym Marceli Weron, and to the editors and publisher of *Schulz/Forum 14*, whose republished copy served as the basis for his translation.

Undula

IT must've been weeks now, months, since I've been locked up in isolation. Over and over I sink into slumber and rouse myself anew, and real-life phantoms get jumbled up, blurring into drowsy figments. So the time passes. It seems I've been living a long time already in this long, crooked room. Sometimes I reacquaint myself with the large, oversized furniture stretching all the way up to the ceiling, the musty wardrobes of simple oak, thick with dust. A large multi-armed chandelier made of dull pewter hangs from the ceiling, swaying slightly.

I lie in the corner of the long yellow bed, scarcely filling a third of it with my body. There are moments in which the room, lit with the lamp's yellow light, disappears somewhere out of sight, and I feel in the leaden inertia of thought only the powerful, calm rhythm of breath, with which my chest steadily rises. And in tandem with this rhythm flows the breath of all things.

Time trickles with the kerosene lamp's faint hissing. Old equipment rattles and creaks in the silence. Besides me in the depths of the room there are the shadows, pointy, crooked, in shards, who skulk and scheme. They stretch out their long necks and peer over my shoulder. I don't turn around. Why should I? As soon as I look they'll all quiet down again in their own place, just a floorboard somewhere will groan, the old wardrobe will creak. Everything will go back to the way it was before. Unchanged. And silence once more, and the old lamp will sweeten the boredom with its lulling hiss.

Big black cockroaches stand motionless and blankly stare into the light. They appear lifeless. Suddenly their flat, headless shells start scuttling in a weird crablike race, cutting diagonally across the floor.

I sleep and wake up and drift off again, and still I patiently wade through the diseased thicket of phantoms and dreams. They thrash about and get tangled together, and with me they roam the muted, off-white jumbled maze, like the pale, nocturnal potato sprouts in the cellar, like the monstrous tumors of diseased mushrooms.

———••———

Maybe it's already spring out there. I don't know how many days and nights have come and gone since that time… I remember that gray, leaden February dawn, that purple procession of bacchants. Thro' a handful of pale squandered nights, right through the moonlit suburban parks, didn't I dash after them like a moth enchanted by Undula's smile. And everywhere in the arms of dancers I saw her, deliciously swooning and careening Undula in black gauze and lingerie, Undula with blazing eyes behind the black lace of a fan. So I followed after her with a sweet, burning fury in my heart until my faint legs no longer wanted to carry me, and the carnival spat me out half-dead onto some empty street in the thick predawn darkening.

My pilgrimage, a groping in the dark, with sleep weighing on my eyelids, up some old stairs, climbing right up thro' the many dark flights, crossing the attic's black expanse, scrambling alongside the rafters overhead, swaying in the dark wind gusts, until at long last a certain secluded corridor sucked me in, where I found myself at the entrance to the apartment from my childhood. I turned the door handle, and with a dark sigh the door opened to the apartment's interior. The smell of those forgotten recesses enfolded me; our former maid Adela quietly stepped out from the depths of the apartment, treading noiselessly in velvet, cork-soled slippers. How pretty she had grown during my absence, how pearly white her shoulders were beneath the black unfastened gown. She wasn't surprised in the least by my entrance after so many years, she was sleepy, curt even. I noticed once more her slender legs with their swanlike silhouette, receding back into the black depth of the apartment.

I groped in the dim light until I found an unmade bed, and with eyes bedimmed by slumber I drowned my face in the pillows.

A muffled dream rolled over me like a heavy cart loaded with the soot of darkness, and it buried me in gloom.

Then the wintry night began to wall itself up with the black brick of nothingness. The endless expanse froze into a blind, deaf crag, into a heavy, impenetrable mass scabbing over the spaces between things, and the world hardened into nothingness.

———••———

How hard it is to breathe in a room caught in the grip of a wintry night. Through the walls and roof one feels the dark pressure of a thousand starless skies. The air is sterile; it hurts my lungs. Even the lamp's flame is overgrown with black mold. The pulse grows weak. Shallow. *T e - d i - u m.* – Someplace deep in the solid mass of night people unaccompanied save for their lanterns make their way down winter's black corridors. It seems like their desperate conversations, their indifferent, monotonous gossip comes flying at me. Undula, Undula lies resting in her own sweet-smelling bed in the embrace of a heavy dream that sucks out from her the memory of all the orgies, of all her follies. With her limp, supple body, unswathed from the constraints of gauze, lingerie, and stockings, she brought darkness to its knees like a great ursine beast wrapped in fur, clutching it in her four enormous paws, gathering to her its creamy, silken appendages into one sweet, yielding handful that she laps up with her scarlet tongue. But she is callous, with eyes far-off in dreams, she surrenders, helpless, to feed upon the darkness, and through her rosy veins flow the milky ways of stars, her eyes drunk on these dizzying carnival nights.

Undula, Undula, thou sighing of the soul into the land of the happy and the beautiful! How my soul has expanded with your radiance, while I stood, a lowly, pitiable Lazarus before your luminous threshold. Through you, in the warm shiver of pleasure, I've come to know my misery and ugliness in the light of your perfection. How sweet it was to read from a single glance the verdict condemning me forevermore, with the most profound humility to submit to the flick of your hand that cast me from your banquet tables. I would've doubted your perfection should you have done otherwise. – Now it's time for me to return to the threshing floor from which I had left only an impetuous miscarriage. I shall follow through to the end so as to atone for being my Maker's mistake.

Undula, Undula! Lucid dream of yon land, before long even I will forsake you. The final darkness draws near, so too, the agony of the threshing floor.

———••———

The lamp hisses boredom and spits and sputters its own monotonous song. It's as though I had heard that song once a very long time ago, somewhere at the start of my life, when I, a sickly infant, tossing and turning, would've been fussy and whining through long, tear-filled nights. Who was it that called out to me back then? Who was it that turned away while I gropingly would've been looking for some kind of path back home to a maternal pre-nothingness?

How the lamp fumes. Gray limbs of the candelabrum sprout like a polyp from the ceiling. The shadows collude and conspire. Cockroaches dart noiselessly across the yellow floor. My bed is so long that I cannot see the opposite end. I'm undeniably sick, gravely so. How bitter and full of agony is the way to the threshing floor.

It had begun then. These monotonous, pointless dialogues with my pain exhausted me through and through. I'd constantly argue with him, that he had no regard for me at all as pure intellect. – And as everything else gets more and more muddled and confused, I unmistakably feel more and more that being under his watch has released me from my suffering. Yet at the same time I feel a slight shiver of dread.

The lamp's flame burns ever lower, ever darker. The shadows stretch out their giraffe-like necks all the way up to the ceiling. They want to catch a glimpse of him, but I carefully tuck him under the duvet. He's like a small, shapeless embryo, with neither face, eyes, nor mouth, and he was born so as to suffer. From life he knows but suffering's shapes and monsters, those which he's come to know in the deep night into which he's been plunged. His senses are turned inward; they greedily seize pain in all its forms. He has taken my suffering upon himself. Sometimes it's as if he's merely some sort of large fish swollen with the searing pain of a hook caught in his tender gill.

Why do you weep and whimper incessantly all night long? How am I supposed to ease your suffering, my little sidekick? What am I to do with you? Where to begin? You squirm, scowl, and twitch. You neither hear nor comprehend human speech, and what's more, you're fussy; your monotonous pain whinges the night long. Now you're like an umbilical cord, coiled up, twisted, and pulsing...

━━ •• ━━

The lamp must've gone out while I was dozing. It's dark and quiet. Nobody's crying. Nothing hurts. Somewhere far off in the depths of the darkness, somewhere behind the wall the gutters are chattering. God! it's thawing!... The attic spaces rumble hollowly like cases of huge musical instruments. In the solid crag of this black winter, the first crack must've formed. The colossal blocks of darkness in the bulwark of night unclench and begin to crumble. The darkness streams out like ink through the fissures of winter, sputtering in the gutters and down the drains. God! spring advances...

Out there in the world the city gradually wrests itself from the fetters of darkness. A thaw carves out house after house from the lithic wall of darkness. Oh, to once more seek advice from the dark breasts of the thawing breath; oh, if only to feel on my face the wind's black damp sails gliding down the streets. The small flickering of the streetlamps on the corner blush ablaze and turn blue as the wind's purple sails fly past. Oh, if only to sneak out and escape, to abandon him here all alone forever with his pain everlasting... What base temptations you are whispering in my ear, o thawing zephyr. But in which part of the city does this apartment lie? Where does this shuttered, boarded-up window lead? As for myself, I can no longer remember the street where my childhood home was. Oh, if only to peek out through the window, to seek guidance from the thawing breeze...

TRANSLATOR'S AFTERWORD

How rare it is to be able to translate into English a long-ago, lost short story by one of the great modernists of European fiction. Knowing that this was a previously unknown, early work, perhaps even Bruno Schulz's literary debut, it was freeing in some sense to be able to set aside not only his other better-known publications but also all subsequent scholarly research as I set about to translate. This story remains mercifully untroubled by what followed its publication: social and political upheavals, war and genocide, the author's own murder, to say nothing of nearly a century of academic work, official editions, and ever greater intellectual handwringing over, and handwashing of, the term *modernism* itself. After all, "Undula" was a literary work less burdened than we by the twentieth century.

Bruno Schulz (1892–1942) was born in the town of Drohobych, Galicia, on the northern slopes of the Carpathian Mountains. In the mid-nineteenth century Drohobych had become Europe's largest oil extraction center, and we have the Galician oil industry, among others, to thank for the preservation and recent discovery of "Undula." Despite living in the town of his birth for most of his fifty years, Schulz found himself an inhabitant of the Austro-Hungarian Empire, the West Ukrainian People's Republic, the Second Polish Republic, Soviet Ukraine, and finally, and fatally, under Nazi Germany occupation. Although Drohobych is now located in Ukraine, it was part of Poland in 1922 when Schulz, aged twenty-nine, published this story in *Dawn: The Journal of Petroleum Officials in Boryslav* [*Świt. Organ urzędników naftowych w Borysławiu*].

The ever-shifting region of Galicia was situated in central-eastern Europe and is today divided between western Ukraine and eastern Poland. The Kingdom of Galicia was created in 1772 with the First Partition of

Poland, which divided the Polish-Lithuanian
Commonwealth, the largest European state
at the time, among Prussia, Russia, and
Austria. For the most part, ethnic minorities
fared better under Austrian rule. The region's
administrative capital was Lviv, known by its
German name Lemberg at the time, located
about eighty kilometers or fifty miles from
Drohobych. The capital became an important
center of Polish, Ukrainian, and Jewish
cultures. In addition to Schulz, Galicia gave
rise to many prominent writers, including,
among others, Ivan Franko, Shmuel Yosef
Agnon, Joseph Roth, Jozef Wittlin, Stanisław
Lem, and Leopold von Sacher-Masoch, who
would exert the most influence on Schulz's
"Undula."

Despite its original publication in 1922,
the story begins with a sentence that reads like
it could have been written in 2020: "It must've
been weeks now, months, since I've been
locked up in isolation." Readers of Schulz will
recognize the character of the maid Adela.
They will identify certain Schulzian themes
and vocabulary: among them, cockroaches,

the hazy borders between dreams and waking life, nostalgia, masochistic eroticism, and references to the Demiurge, which I translate as Maker. So many of the themes and images that appear throughout Schulz's writings also appear here in what seems to be, as far as we can tell, his first literary publication. As Lesya Khomych notes, in this one story we find the confluence of images from his artwork and literary images from his later writings.

Admirers of Schulz's visual art will recognize the name Undula from a series, also from the early 1920s, of slightly erotic cliché-verre works published as *The Book of Idolatry* [*Xięga Bałwochwalcża*]. (In addition to *idolatrous, bałwochwalcża* can also be translated as *slavish*.) It has been claimed that these prints, some of which are held by the National Museum in Krakow, were to illustrate a new edition of Sacher-Masoch's *Venus in Furs*, first translated into Polish in 1913. The series depicts a man often groveling before a dominant woman wearing a blasé expression, and individual images seem to illustrate specific scenes from Sacher-Masoch's novel.

It was while conducting research in Lviv's Vasyl Stefanyk National Scientific Library on reviews of an art show where Schulz exhibited some of his work for *The Book of Idolatry* that Khomych came across a short story that shared its unusual name with a woman featured in the artwork. The story had been published under the name Marceli Weron, but it was unmistakably the work of Bruno Schulz.

Like the Polish word *undyna*, the name Undula refers to the undine or the ondine, beings beget of water. The name can be traced back to the Latin *unda*, meaning *wave*, and it shares its root with *undulant* and *undulate*. Undula, then, means little wave or wavelet. We can imagine an allusion, no matter how slight, to Warsaw's symbol of the sword-wielding mermaid, who has appeared on the city's coat of arms since the early seventeenth century.

But Undula did not spring fully formed in Schulz's imagination. We can trace her lineage back to the Greek goddess Venus and to the Russian Tsarina Catherine the Great by way of Sacher-Masoch's own heroine Wanda von Dunajew, who appears in his novel as a Venus, albeit one wrapped in furs. And what a name: *Dunajew*, with its nod toward the Dunaj, the Slavic name for the Danube River (Danube itself meaning something like born of dew) and ending with *jew*, pronounced *yev*, but gesturing, at least in English, toward *Jew*. Undula's wavelet seems to likewise pay homage to the watery Dunajew, who in effect is a descendant of the Danube, which is what her name would mean in Russian. Yet she has a noble title, and one that is distinctly German: *von* Dunajew, making her name at once both eastern and western, both entitled master and (Danubian) Jew.

In addition to the overt theme of masochism, "Undula" echoes with other Symbolist and Decadent motifs. Schulz emphasizes dreams and phantoms throughout the story. The narrator's pain manifests as a homunculus. As in his later stories, objects are unleashed from their backgrounds; they change and transform further as they are perceived by the narrator. In turn, what could easily have remained in the background as mere setting shifts to the foreground. The setting in effect becomes subject matter, destabilizing the story's, the character's, the narrator's tenuous grasp on time-space.

Notwithstanding the contemporary tone of its opening sentence, "Undula" reads as if it could have been written somewhere between a Gothic-tinged descent into madness à la Edgar Allan Poe and some debauched revelry by Joris-Karl Huysmans, which is one reason why I chose a pseudo-elevated, quasi-archaic register in English. Schulz's use of the obsolete Polish preposition *skróś* helped to validate this interpretation choice. Because this preposition is more at home in the poetry of Adam Mickiewicz (1798–1855), Schulz reveals himself to be firmly established in the even longer nineteenth century. I translate it with the archaic and hyper-literary English *thro'*.

Perhaps the most drastic choice I made as translator was in rendering *retorta*. A retort is a large steel furnace for burning charcoal, usually in a forest setting. Since the entirety of the story's action takes place indoors, it seems unlikely Schulz was referring to this kind of *retorta*. But there is a different kind as well, a spherical type of vessel, usually made of glass or copper, used in the alchemical purification process and also still used for distillation. It seems likely that Schulz, whose heroine Undula was named for the undines who were first mentioned in an alchemical treatise by Paracelsus, was as familiar with these kinds of retorts as he would have been with the industry-scale versions used in oil extraction. Conceivably, our narrator was being kept in some kind of building that housed an alchemical laboratory. But just how many English readers would understand what this kind of equipment was?

Simplifying and reducing *retort* to *oven* or *furnace* seemed to impose too much of an overly complicated context onto a Polish short story by a Jewish author before World War II. So I was tasked with finding a suitable word that could convey an industrial, mechanical process of purification, which can be read both literally—he hears equipment creak—as well as figuratively—he returns to the retort in order to be purified, to be made more perfect. *Crucible*, which reads more metaphorical than actual, was not an option. *Mortar and pestle*, which followed this line of thought, made it sound like the narrator was going to the kitchen to prepare a meal.

Reimagining the purification processes, both technical and figurative, led me to something that has ties to the Bible (twenty-six references in total) as well as to BDSM. A threshing floor could be located indoors, and before the invention of threshing machines, the process involved a flail, a type of whip used to thresh grain and goad livestock, as a weapon in battle, and lastly, at least since the time of Sacher-Masoch, as a piece of equipment in BDSM erotic role-playing. This comprehensible solution also provided a constellation of implications that seemed to best match the tone and themes of the story.

Finally, I would like to mention just one passage among many where it appears Schulz was using language in a particularly original way. In Polish there is the stock phrase *spędzać sen z powiek*, which usually means something

23

like *to spend a sleepless night*, though a more verbatim translation might be *to drive away sleep/a dream from (one's) eyelids*. In "Undula," Schulz writes, *ze snem na powiekach* [verbatim: *with sleep/a dream on (one's) eyelids*], which I expressed as *with sleep weighing on my eyelids*. Schulz overturns the stock phrase's meaning by shifting from the genitive *z powiek* to the locative *na powiekach*, and instead of *sen* being in the accusative case, as it is commonly, he instrumentalizes it by writing *ze snem*. To a native speaker of Polish, this might not be of any interest at all, but to a non-native grammar enthusiast, it is compelling to see how Schulz manipulates and makes pliable his native language.

Thank you for reading.

ACKNOWLEDGMENTS

With gratitude to Melissa Beck, Stanley Bill, Stephen Harding, Matthew Jakubowski, Jakub Orzeszek, Joshua Rothes, and Jola Zandecki.

ABOUT THE AUTHOR

Bruno Schulz (1892—1942) was a Jewish author, artist, critic, and teacher from Drohobych, which at the time of his birth was a town in Austrian Galicia. Widely renowned as one of the twentieth century's greatest prose stylists, Schulz left behind only a small body of work, including two collections of short stories, as well as assorted letters, essays, and a handful of additional pieces of short fiction. Schulz was shot and killed in 1942 by a Gestapo officer while returning to the Drohobych Ghetto carrying a loaf of bread. Tragically, many of his final works have been lost, including the fabled novel *The Messiah*.

ABOUT THE TRANSLATOR

Frank Garrett holds a PhD in philosophy and literary theory. He trained as a translator at the Center for Translation Studies at the University of Texas at Dallas and at Philipps-Universität Marburg after earning advanced certification in Polish philology from the Catholic University of Lublin. In 2000 he was a FLAS fellow at the Ivan Franko National University of Lviv, and in 2001 he was a Fulbright scholar in Warsaw. His work has been published by, among others, Black Sun Lit, Burning House Press, Duquesne UP, Spurl Editions, and Zeta Books, and has appeared in *3:AM Magazine*, *Transitions Online*, and *minor literature[s]*, where he serves as a contributing editor. Outpost19 published his translation of Robert Rient's memoir *Witness* in 2016. Frank lives in Dallas with his husband.

Sublunary Editions is a small, independent press based in Seattle, Washington. It publishes short books of innovative writing from a worldwide cadre of authors, past and present. Subscriptions are available at:
subeds.com/subscribe

OTHER SUBLUNARY EDITIONS TITLES

Falstaff: Apotheosis
Pierre Senges (translated by Jacob Siefring)

926 Years
Kyle Coma-Thompson, Tristan Foster

Corpses
Vik Shirley

A Luminous History of the Palm
Jessica Sequeira

The Wreck of the Large Glass / Paleódromo
Mónica Belevan

Under the Sign of the Labyrinth
Christina Tudor-Sideri

MARCELI WERON.
(Przedruk i przekład bez zezwolenie Redakcji wzbroniony).

UNDULA.

Musiały już upłynąć tygodnie, miesiące, od kiedy zamknięty jestem w tej samotni. Zapadam wciąż na nowo w sen i znów się budzę i majaki jawy plączą się z wytworami omroczy sennej. Tak upływa — czas. Zdaje mi się, że w tym długim krzywym pokoju już kiedyś dawno mieszkałem. Czasem odpoznaję te nad miarę wielkie meble sięgające do sufitu, te szafy z prostego dębu, najeżone zakurzonymi gratami. Wielka, wieloramienna lampa z szarej cyny zwiesza się ze stropu, kołysząc się z lekka.

Leżę w rogu długiego żółtego łóżka, wypełniając zaledwie trzecią jego część mem ciałem. Są chwile, w których pokój oświetlony żółtem światłem lampy ginie mi gdzieś z oczu i czuję tylko w ciężkim bezwładzie myśli potężny spokojny rytm oddechu, którym moja pierś się miarowo podnosi. I w zgodzie z tym rytmem idzie oddech wszystkich rzeczy.

Sączy się czas mdłem syczeniem lampy naftowej. Stare sprzęty trzaskają i trzeszczą w ciszy. Poza mną w głębi pokoju czają się i spiskują cienie, śpiczaste, krzywe, połamane. Wyciągają długie szyje i zaglądają mi poprzez ramiona. Nie odwracam się. I pocóżby?